LUNAR JIM

Annual 2008

Contents

Meet our friends from MOONA LUNA!

Hello everybody! I'm Jim and I'm an explorer! Let's get lunar and solve some moon mysteries together!

This is my robot dog, ROVER. He only makes beeps and blips, but I can understand him! He helps me on my missions and loves adventures!

Walk your fingers along the path

Wave hello as you go past!

T.E.D.

Lunar Jim

ROVER

4

Moon Facts

Earth's moon is very similar to the moon where my friends and I live. Here are some fun facts about it!

The gravitational pull of the moon creates the waves in the sea.

The moon is the second brightest object in our sky after the sun.

Things weigh less on the moon than they do on Earth.

The moon travels around the planet Earth in a circle called an orbit.

You can only see the same side of the moon from Earth.

The moon has no atmosphere, which means it would be hard to walk around without a special spacesuit like Jim's!

Space Fact:

Moon dust is formed from the impact of meteors upon its surface.

It's one-quarter the size our planet.

My Moon Diary

The moon takes about 29 days to travel around the planet Earth. Ask an adult to help you keep a diary of its different phases!

Phase		Date	My drawing
New Moon	⬤	....	◯
First quarter	◖	....	◯
Full Moon	◯	....	◯
Last quarter	◗	....	◯

You can use a crayon or coloured pencil to draw your own moon in the box on the right. Don't be afraid to ask for help!

HELP

Help T.E.D. count the objects below and write your answers in the spaces provided!

Mission 1

How many **lunar worms** do you see?

Your answer

Mission 2

How many **moon melons** do you see?

Your answer

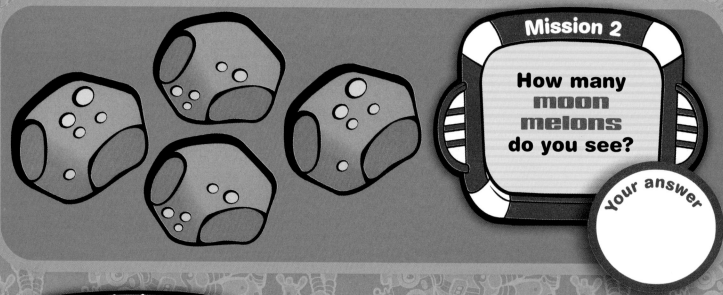

Mission 3

How many times do you see **Dolores**?

Your answer

T.E.D.!

Help **T.E.D.** tick the right boxes!

Mission 4

Which is the biggest **planet?**

a. ☐   b. ☐   c. ☐

a. ☐   b. ☐   c. ☐

Mission 5

Which is the smallest **blue moon banana?**

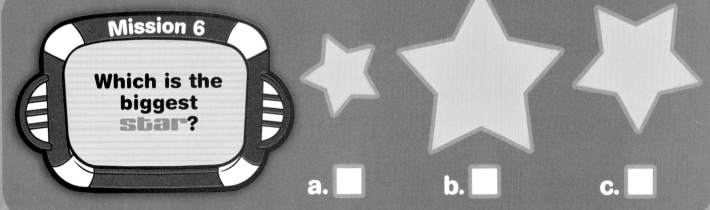

Mission 6

Which is the biggest **star?**

a. ☐   b. ☐   c. ☐

spot the difference

There are **three** differences to spot between the two pictures, can you find them all?

The differences in the second picture are: Jim's flower is yellow, Daisy's bell is red, and there's a light missing from above Jim's head!

Colouring in time!

Use your favourite coloured pencils and crayons to colour in this picture of **Jim** and **Rover**!

Don't be afraid to use your imagination!

That Sinking Feeling

Hello everyone! It's story time! In space, it's hard to keep your feet on the ground... as Rover and I found out in this adventure!

One afternoon, Jim was playing catch with Rover. "Okay, Rover! Here goes! Ready to catch the ball?" he said. Rover bleeped that he was, and Jim threw the ball high into the air. Suddenly, there was a loud **crash**.

"Ooops!" Jim said to himself. "Now I remember why I made up that rule about not playing ball in the house!" At that moment, Pixel appeared on the View Comm.

"Jim, my data reports there was a lunar dust storm in Sector 8 last night."

"**Great galaxies!**" exclaimed Jim. "Playtime's over, Rover! To the control tower!"

Outside the tower, Ripple was adjusting a small satellite dish. "Jumping Jupiter, that's very shiny!" said Jim as he approached.

"Are you going to Sector 8, Jim?" asked Ripple.

"Yes. In fact, I'm going to investigate the dust storm!" Jim replied.

"I'll join you," Ripple said. "That's where I have to set up the satellite dish."

"Let's get this **mission** started!" said Jim triumphantly.

Jim threw the ball high into the air. Suddenly, there was a loud crash.

"Did somebody say 'mission?'" asked T.E.D., who had magically appeared from behind the tower. Without a word of warning, T.E.D. fell over backwards onto the ground.

"Ahh! My visualising circuits! I can't see!" he cried as he lay in a big pile of **lunar dust**.

"It's just the satellite dish, T.E.D. It's so shiny, the light reflects off it like a flashlight," said Ripple sympathetically.

As Jim and Ripple helped him up, T.E.D. looked stunned.

"I feel dizzy! I think Ripple will have to give me a complete check up!"

"I can only do that if you are able to set up the satellite for me, Jim," said Ripple.

"Roger that! **Let's get Lunar!**" said Jim, and in less time than it takes for a comet to fly past your eyes, he was whooshing down the chute into the prep pad area where his boots, helmet and gloves were waiting for him. With a quick wipe of Rover's eyes, they were off to the vehicle prep area where they hopped into the **Lunar crawler**.

"The grappler attachment can carry Ripple's satellite dish, Rover," Jim said as they sped along the dusty moon terrain towards Sector 8. When they arrived, Jim was amazed by what he saw.

"Look at that!" he exclaimed. "The crater's are all filled with lunar dust!"

Jim began to unhook the satellite, which flashed under the brightness of the sun above. All of a sudden, Rover's ball rolled past Jim's feet, followed by one very excitable robot dog.

"Woah! **slow down**, Rover!" shouted Jim after his friend. Rover's ball came to rest in the centre of a lunar dust crater, held for a moment, and then began to sink down slowly.

"That lunar dust pool is just like quicksand back on Earth!" said Jim. "It's a good thing you didn't follow it in there!"

Rover barked as Jim gave him a big hug. His tail began to wag happily. But as Jim stood up, the remote control for the satellite fell from his glove and broke on the ground. With a mechanical whir, the satellite powered up and its huge dish began to pivot. The glare from the sun reflected directly into Jim's eyes, blinding him. As he stepped back shielding his eyes, the ground beneath his feet became just that little bit softer…

Back at the control tower, Ripple was examining T.E.D., who was still

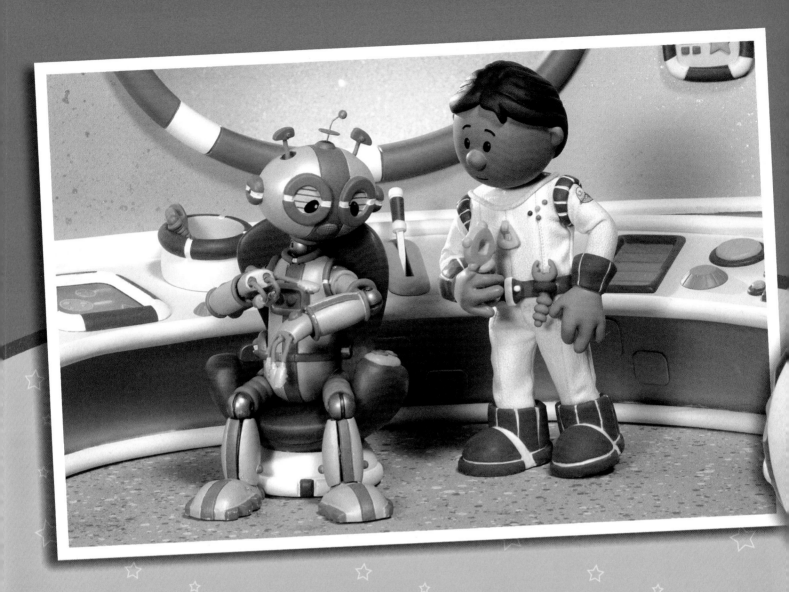

complaining about his ailments. Looking over her clipboard once again, she shook her head in disbelief.

"Let me sit down before you give me the bad news!" said T.E.D., with a little bit of fear in his voice. Ripple sighed.

"Everything seems to be in perfect working order, T.E.D.," said Ripple.

"Then how come I feel more dizzy that before?" he replied.

"There's absolutely nothing wrong with you," said Ripple.

Ted suddenly jumped to his feet.

"If that's so, why am I seeing strange flashes?" T.E.D. bleeted.

"You're seeing flashes?" asked Ripple. T.E.D. pointed out of the window to where he could see bright pulses on the horizon.

"Wait T.E.D.! That flashing is coming from Sector 8! That's where Jim went!" Ripple turned on her View Comm and tried to contact Jim, but there was no answer.

"Jim's not responding, Ripple," announced Pixel.

"He must be in **trouble!** Come on T.E.D.!" Within moments, she had launched her scooter, and took off at high speed towards Sector 8 to find Jim. T.E.D. was hanging on the back of it for dear life.

As they approached the satellite,

said, producing Rover's ball from behind his back. Rover barked excitedly.

"I'm not surprised you had something to do with this **calamity!**" said T.E.D. to Rover, who was running around with his newly found toy. "Thankfully, my perfect vision saved the day!"

Just as he spoke, T.E.D. fell backwards over Ripple's scooter.

"Ow!" he groaned. "Ripple... I think I need another check up!"

they could see Jim sitting halfway up to his waste in the lunar dust.

"We saw your signal, are you alright, Jim?" asked Ripple, as she got off her scooter.

"Yes, but you could say I'm in a bit of a sticky situation!" he replied, and they both exchanged a grin.

"Leave it to me!" said Ripple. Using the grappler arm from the Lunar Crawler, Ripple lifted Jim from the pool of lunar dust.

"Phew! Thanks Ripple. And guess what I found when I was stuck in the dust, Rover?" Jim

Ripple lifted Jim from the pool of lunar dust.

Adapted by JP Rutter from the episode written by Pete Sauder

VEHICLES

Let me drive!

If I need to find something in a dark place, I use the

LUNAR CRAWLER WITH SEARCHER

Let's get Lunar!

When I'm in a hurry, I zoom about on my

LUNAR SCRAMBLER

memory quiz!

Look at the picture of Jim and Rover for 30 seconds, cover it up with a piece of paper, and see how many questions you can answer correctly in the spaces provided!

1. What is Jim holding in his hand?

2. Who is Jim talking to?

3. What colour is the window frame?

4. What colour are Rover's ears?

5. What is wrapping around Jim's chair?

Answers: 1. A magnet, 2. Rover, 3. Blue, 4. Yellow, 5. Vine.

Lunar Numbers

Can you count as high as Ripple?

9 Nine

10 Ten

11 Eleven

12 Twelve

8 Eight

4 Four

5 Five

6 Six

7 Seven

3 Three

1 One

2 Two

Every time you see a picture, **shout** out the name or the words.

Jim   **Eco**   **Rover**   **Pixel**

"Mmm, there's nothing as tasty as your lunar donuts, !" said  to his friend. "Watch this, !"  replied, and dropped the donut onto the ground. With a BOING noise, it began to bounce all around 's kitchen. "At least  likes them," said  as he watched his robot friend scamper after it. "What did you make them with?" asked . "Lunar rubber tree jelly! I ran out of flour," said , with a smile on his face. "We're running out of

everything," replied , "the supply pod's never been so late!" The wild donut bounced into the air once more, and  caught it on his tail. "Nice catch!" said . "Let's see if  knows anything about the supply pod." 's screen lit up at the mention of her name. "? Any idea when the supply pod might arrive?" asked . "My radar reports it has already begun landing procedures," replied . "Jumping Jupiter! That's great news!" said . "Let's get Lunar!" And with that,  and his friend  rushed off to begin another adventure!

Adapted by JP Rutter from the episode written by Bruce Robb

ANSWERS: 1. Eco, 2. Dolores, 3. Lunar Jim, 4. Rover, 5. Lunar Worm, 6. Daisy, 7. Ripple

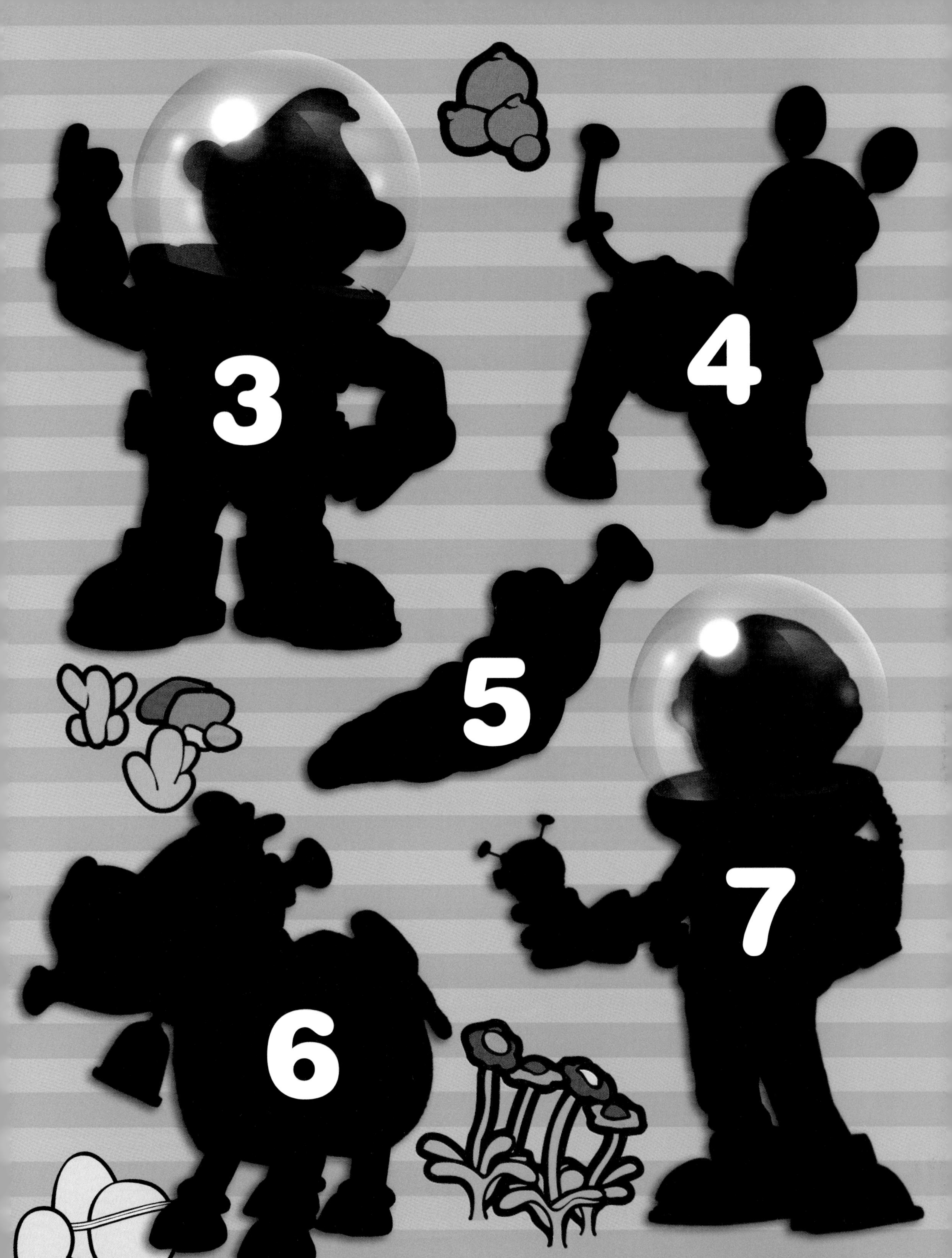

Lunar

Let Ripple teach you

a is for
alien

b is for
blue

c is for
Colby

d is for
Daisy

i is for
invent

j is for
Jim

k is for
kind

l is Lunar
Lifter

r is for
Ripple

s is for
Scrambler

t is for
T.E.D.

alphabet

your lunar A, B, C, and D's!

e is for Eco

f is for fly

g is for gravity

h is for Hopper

m is for moon

n is for night

o is for orbit

p is for Pixel

q is for quick

u is for up

v is for vine

w is for worm

x is for x-ray

y is for you!

z is for zoom

Cowboy Jim

It's story time once again! Eco and I discovered something strange in the Ecodome that soon had us all wrapped up!

"Yee-haw! That was a great cowboy movie we saw last night, Eco!" cried Jim one day in the Ecodome.

"It was!" agreed Eco. "The cowboys were so brave, riding those big horses and lassoing the cows with ropes!"

"These vines you're growing look like ropes, Eco," said Jim, tripping over a large stem.

"Aren't they great? I put some seed in lunar soil and they've grown faster than a **supersonic** rocket!" said Eco.

landed on the pad. **whirr! whirr! whirr!** went the gadgets as they put on Jim's boots, helmet and gloves. **swish! swish! swish!** went the wiper as it cleaned Rover's eyes.

"What vehicle should we take?" asked Jim. "Whatever was making that noise was moving very fast... I know! Let's take the Scrambler!" With a **WHOOSH**, the hatch opened and the Scrambler bobbed out.

"What are they for?" asked Jim.

"They're beanstalks. In a few weeks, there will be some big, delicious beans for us to eat!" explained Eco.

Suddenly, Jim and Eco heard a very strange noise.

"What was that?" wondered Jim.

"He-e-e-e-elp!" went the sound.

"It's a **moon mystery**!" cried Jim. "Come on, Rover, let's get lunar!"

Lunar Jim and Rover hurried to Mission Control. They slid down to the vehicle prep area and

"Help me! I don't want to be put in the bin!" shrieked T.E.D.

Jim and Rover were soon speeding round the Ecodome, looking for what had made the noise.

"He-e-e-elp!" went the sound again.

"Did you hear that, Rover?" asked Jim. "Where's it coming from?"

"BLIP! BLIP! BEEP!" went Rover, pointing with his nose.

"Over there you say, boy?" cried Jim. "Let's go!"

Jim steered the Scrambler towards the place Rover's nose was pointing to.

"Great galaxies! It's T.E.D.!" exclaimed Jim. "He's being chased!"

"Ooh! Thank you for saving me, Jim!" said T.E.D.

"Help me, Jim!" shrieked T.E.D. "Ripple's spring-cleaning machine has robo-fleas in its floppy drive! It thinks I'm a piece of junk and it keeps trying to throw me in the bin. Yikes! Here it comes again!"

"Jumping Jupiter! We'd better think of something quick, Rover!" cried Jim.

"BEEP! BEEP! BLIP!" barked Rover.

"Yes, a rope! Then we could lasso the machine just like the cowboys in that movie!" said Jim. "But where will we find a rope long enough?"

"BLIP!" beeped Rover.

"The vines?" said Jim. "Of course, Eco's beanstalks! They looked just like ropes, didn't they!"

Jim raced to the Ecodome.

"I need one of your beanstalks, Eco!" he called.

"This should do," said Eco, cutting the longest beanstalk he could find.

Jim tied the stalk into a lasso and scrambled to save T.E.D.

"Yee-ha!" he cried, as he swung the lasso round his head and roped the machine. "Gotcha!"

"Oh my!" T.E.D. panted. "Thank you, Jim… although, five more minutes and I would have stopped that maniac machine myself!"

"Of course you would have, T.E.D.!" laughed Jim.

Story written by Jennifer Anstruther

Where's

Rover?

Rover's gotten himself lost! Can you see him anywhere? Write the name of any other objects you can find in the box below.

Rover is hiding ....

Other objects I can see are:

....

....

....

....

....

Answer: Rover is hiding behind the big rock on the left page.

33

Learn

I've been learning about how things change when they are very **COLD**, and what happens when they get **WARM** again. Try this experiment to see for yourself.

You'll need:
Water
Two paper cups
Ice lolly sticks
A grown-up

- Fill the cups with water.
- Put them in the freezer. Check every 10 minutes to see what's happening.

- When they are just starting to freeze, put in the ice lolly sticks.
- Once they have frozen, take them out of the freezer.
- Peel the cups off both lollies.

with Jim!

- Put one ice lolly on a plate and leave it on a sunny window ledge.
- Watch and you will see the ice turn back into water as it gets warm.

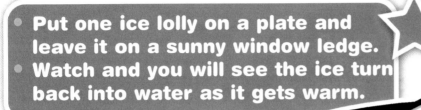

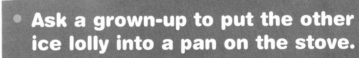

- Ask a grown-up to put the other ice lolly into a pan on the stove.
- Now watch what happens.
- Can you see the steam? When water is very hot it turns into a vapour, which is like a gas.

I learned that when some things get very **HOT** or very **COLD**, they can change from a liquid like water into a solid like ice, or into a gas like steam. Did you learn this too?

MOON GOPHER

fluffies

pixie

Rhyme

Can you help me finish these rhymes? Ask a grown up to help you trace the words with a pencil, then draw a picture of the word in the box beside it!

This funny-looking purple stone,

Reminds me of an ice-cream cone.

I made a brilliant rhyme!

This stinky, smelly, yucky lake,

Is making Jim's poor nostrils ache!

I did it again! I'm a genius!

Noisy plants go pop, pop, pop,

They make me want to blow my top!

This is my best one yet!

Oh! I'm starting to shiver and shake,

I think I saw a stripy space snake.

I'm so clever!

with T.E.D.!

Lunar Dust Storm

Strange things are happening in Moona Luna! Why not get comfortable and let this fantastic story blow you away!

It was a windy day on Blue Moon L22. Jim was out in the Lunar Crawler collecting moon rocks with Rover. All of a sudden, he noticed a dark cloud heading straight towards Moona Luna.

"Hmm, I don't like the look of that," said Jim, peering through his telescope. "Just as I thought! It's a lunar dust storm! We had better stay in the Lunar Crawler until it blows past, Rover."

"**BEEP!**" said Rover, settling down under Jim's seat.

After a few minutes the storm was blasting through Moona Luna with great speed, covering everything with a layer of dust. When Jim was sure it was all over, he and Rover stepped out of the Lunar Crawler to inspect the village.

"First things first, let's get back to Mission Control!" said Jim.

Back at Mission Control, everything seemed fine, but Ripple was nowhere to be seen! Pixel replied that she hadn't seen her all morning. Jim lept into action.

"Come on Rover, **let's get lunar** and find Ripple!"

Outside, Moona Luna had been transformed into a collection of odd shapes and figures all covered in lunar dust. Soon, Jim and Rover came across a shape that was the same height as Ripple.

"**Quick Rover**," said Jim. "Help me get the dust off!"

But, as the dust flew off, Jim saw that it wasn't Ripple after all. It was just a tall pile of moon rocks!

"**oh dear**, that's not Ripple!

Let's keep searching, Rover!" said Jim.

After a few more steps, Jim and Rover discovered another lunar dust-covered shape.

"Hmm, this one looks like it has arms and legs. Let's try again," said Jim.

This time, as they blew the dust off the figure, Jim saw a familiar face he thought he recognised. It wasn't Ripple after all, but their robotic friend, T.E.D.!

"Oh my! Thank goodness for that!" said T.E.D. "I think I would have

turned into a statue if I had stayed like that for much longer!"

T.E.D. hadn't seen Ripple either, so the three of them continued to search.

"There's only one place left," said Jim. "**THE ECODOME!**"

At the Ecodome, Eco was busy picking moon melons.

"Hello everyone!" he said, cheerfully.

Jim, Rover and T.E.D. looked around the Ecodome, but they couldn't see Ripple anywhere.

"**IT'S NO USE!**" said T.E.D. "Ripple's been lost forever!"

Just then, Jim spotted something familiar behind Eco's Hopper... It was Ripple's tool kit!

"Hello everyone!" said Ripple, as she slid from underneath the Hopper. "What is everyone doing here?"

Jim, Rover and T.E.D. looked confused.

"Haven't you seen? There's been a lunar dust storm and everything is covered with lunar dust!" said Jim.

"**Really!**" said Ripple, surprised.

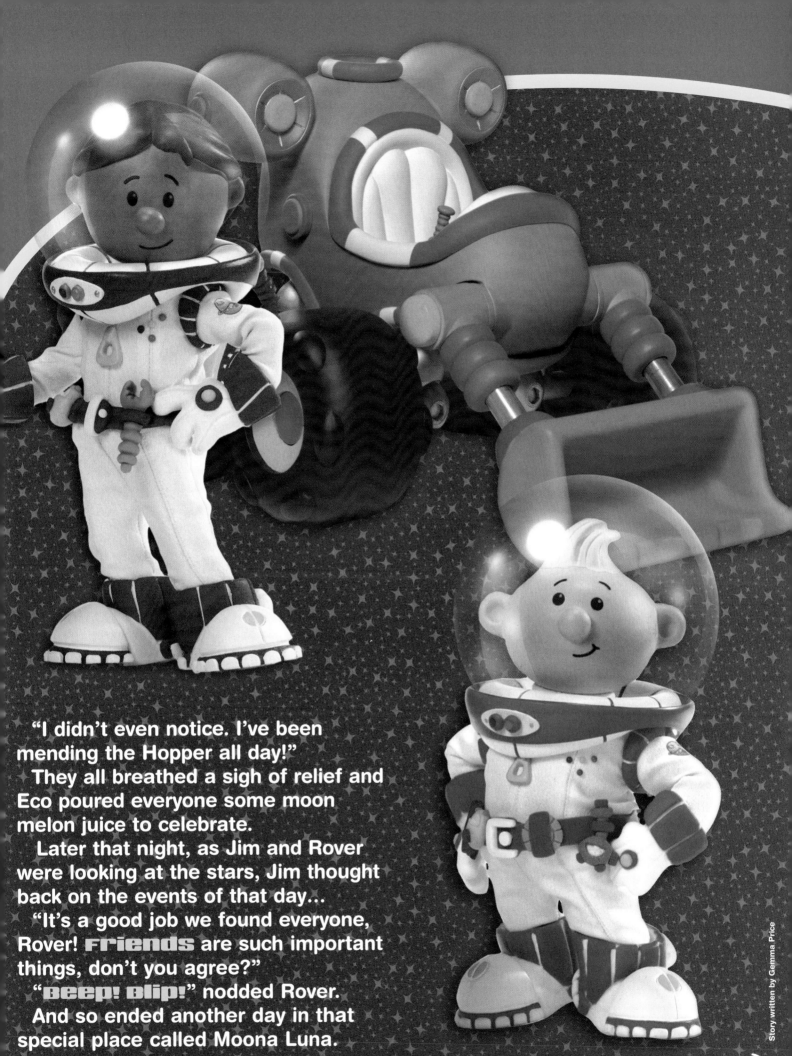

"I didn't even notice. I've been mending the Hopper all day!"

They all breathed a sigh of relief and Eco poured everyone some moon melon juice to celebrate.

Later that night, as Jim and Rover were looking at the stars, Jim thought back on the events of that day...

"It's a good job we found everyone, Rover! **FRIENDS** are such important things, don't you agree?"

"**BEEP! BLIP!**" nodded Rover.

And so ended another day in that special place called Moona Luna.

Story written by Gemma Price

colour

Hello everyone!
Look at the questions on the right and write the name of each colour you see. Answers are at the bottom of the page — but no peeking unless you get stuck!

1

What colour is the flower?

....

matching

2 What colour is Jim's hair?

....

3 What colour is the door behind Eco?

....

4 What colour are Ripple's shoes?

....

5 What colour is Eco's belt?

....

Answer: 1. The flower is PINK, 2. Jim's hair is YELLOW, 3. The door is BLUE, 4. Ripple's shoes are RED, 5. Eco's belt is GREEN.

45

Draw

Trace over the dots to write T.E.D.'S name

T.E.D.

Now it's time to draw! Try copying what's missing from the picture of T.E.D. on this page onto his picture on the right. Have fun!

Colour T.E.D. using the colours at the top of the right page or any other colour you like!

with Ripple

RESCUE T.E.D.!

You will need

A LONG PEN or CHOPSTICK

A SMALL MAGNET

SEVEN SMALL PAPERCLIPS

A PIECE OF STRING

SOME STICKY TAPE

48

Scissor Alert!
Ask a grown-up to help you!

How to play

1 After cutting out all of your characters, attach a magnet to the back of Jim (and Ripple, if there are two of you playing) using sticky tape. Tape a short length of string (20cm) to the top of Jim, and the other end to your pen or chopstick to make a fishing rod.

2 Using sticky tape, put a paperclip on the back of each of the other characters you've cut out, but make sure that you don't cover it up completely with the tape!

3 Get some tin foil from the kitchen and line a deep saucepan with it, making sure you cover the outside. Your pan should now look like a shiny silver cavern!

4 Place your characters into the bottom of the cavern, and using your fishing rod, lower Jim into it slowly and try to pick up T.E.D. If you are playing with a friend, take turns with each other. The first to rescue T.E.D. is the winner!

If you don't want to spoil your annual, ask an adult to make a photocopy of these pages!

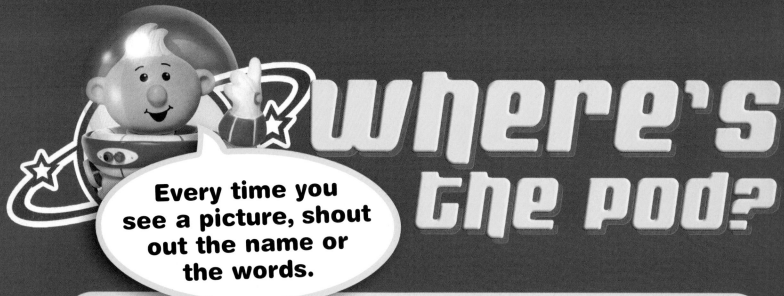

where's the pod?

Every time you see a picture, shout out the name or the words.

Jim   **Eco**   **Rover**   **supply pod**

"Hello, [Jim]!" said [Eco] from the View Comm. "The [supply pod] arrives today and my automatic popcorn plants are on board!" "Just in time for movie night!" said [Jim]. Then his wall monitor beeped. "Pixel here, [Jim] We've lost contact with the [supply pod]!" "Great galaxies!" cried [Jim]. "Lost contact with the popcorn... er, [supply pod]? Come on, [Rover]! Let's get lunar!" [Jim] and [Rover] hurried to Mission Control. "Let's take the Lunar Lifter!" said [Jim]. "Buckle up, [Rover]!" cried [Jim], as they went to find the [supply pod]. On the dark side of the

moon, ___ and ___ saw some tracks. "Hmm... SIX footprints! And drag marks... I think the ___ has been stolen by a six-footed alien!" cried ___ . "Let's follow the tracks!" So, ___ and ___ followed the tracks right into the Ecodome. "Look, boy!" said ___ , pointing to an alien-shaped shadow behind the movie screen! "Ahem... come out, Mr Alien!" cried ___ . "All right! Don't get your space shorts in a twist!" said the alien. "Huh? How does it know I wear space shorts?" thought ___ . "Moo!" said the alien. "Moo?" said ___ . Then ___ and Daisy came out from behind the screen with the ___ . "It's only you!" laughed ___ . "You've found the ___ !" "Yes, and the popcorn's ready for movie night!" said ___ . "See, you're not the only one who can save the day, ___ !"

Adapted by Jennifer Anstruther from the episode 'That's Odd, Where's the Pod', written by Ian James Corlett

Luna!

Draw over the dotted lines to write Pixel's name.

Pixel

My name is **PIXEL** and this is the Mission Control Tower. All the lunar vehicles are kept here.

This is my house. It has a windmill on it so I can make my own electricity.

Dolores the hen lives in the **ECODOME**. Colour in Dolores.

Join the

Join the **stars** to complete the picture. Then colour it in using the colours below.

start here

Now colour the picture using these colours.

stars!

start here →

Now colour the picture using these colours.

Too Many Fluffies

Here's a little story about some amazing creatures we discovered here on the moon! We call them **Fluffies**!

It had been unusually cold on the moon so Jim, Rover and T.E.D. had taken the Lunar Hopper to go and collect the special crystals that give off both light and heat from the **crystal cave**.

"Are w-we t-there yet?" asked T.E.D.

"**Beep Blip!**" barked Rover, pointing at a cave with his nose.

"No, that's not the Crystal Cave, Rover. It must be a cave we haven't explored yet," said Jim.

"Let's explore it n-now! Maybe there are warm crystals inside it too. Or s-something warm. Warm cave bats. I d-don't care as long as it's **warm**!" T.E.D. shivered.

So Rover and Jim went into the cave, but there wasn't a crystal in sight.

"Okay-nothing-warm-here-let's-go!" cried T.E.D., rushing in and out again frantically.

"T.E.D.'s right, Rover!" laughed Jim. "Let's go to the Crystal Cave."

Rover was sniffing at a small fuzz ball on the ground, but at Jim's command, Rover turned and followed him out of the cave. And the fuzz ball followed Rover!

Later, back at the Ecodome, Jim, Rover and T.E.D. were helping Eco put the crystals they'd collected into pots when they heard a **cooing** noise.

"It must have followed us home from the empty cave!" said Jim.

"What's that?" wondered Jim.
Rover sniffed behind a pot and
the fuzz ball from the empty cave
appeared!

"It must have followed us home
from the empty cave!" said Jim.
"I guess we should take it back
first thing in the morning. You can
stay in the Ecodome tonight,
Fluffy!"

The next morning, as Jim was eating
breakfast, his View Comm dropped
down. All he could hear at first was
lots of cooing but then he heard Eco's
voice.

"You'd better come to the Ecodome,
Jim! Quick!" said Eco.

So, Jim and Rover hurried to the Ecodome.

"Where did they all come from?" asked Jim, staring at a pile of Fluffies.

"They're multiplying. First there was one, then two, then four, then eight. Now there are so many, I've lost count!" explained Eco.

"We'd better get them back to the empty cave now before they fill the whole Ecodome!" said Jim.

At the empty cave, Jim put the last of the Fluffies on the floor.

"Mission accomplished!" said Jim. "Brr, it's cold! Let's get back

The only thing they liked was T.E.D.— and his warm crystal.

to Moona Luna where it's warm, Rover!"

Jim and Rover left the empty cave and went back to the Ecodome. But they weren't alone — the Fluffies followed them!

"coo! coo!" they went, back in the Ecodome.

"Oh no! They followed you!" cried Eco. "What are we going to do now?" They tried to get the Fluffies to follow them back to the cave, but that didn't work. They tried to lead them

away with food, but the Fluffies weren't interested. The only thing they liked was T.E.D. — and his warm crystal.

"beep blip!" said Rover.

"I think you're right, Rover! The Fluffies want to stay here because it's warm!" cried Jim.

"What if we gave them some crystals to warm up their cave?" suggested Eco.

"But we don't have enough crystals," said Ripple.

"great galaxies, of course!" cried Jim. "Why don't we just move the Fluffies to the Crystal Cave!"

That's just what they did, and the Fluffies stayed happy, warm and cosy in their new home.

Adapted by Jennifer Anstruther from the episode written by Bruce Robb

GET LUNAR WITH TWO FANTASTIC DVDS

OUT NOW